Karen's Surprise

**Here are some other books
about Karen
that you might enjoy:**

Karen's Witch

Karen's Roller Skates

Karen's Worst Day

Karen's Kittycat Club

Karen's School Picture

Karen's Little Sister

Karen's Birthday

Karen's Haircut

Karen's Sleepover

Karen's Grandmothers

Karen's Prize

Karen's Ghost

Karen's New Year

Little Sister

Karen's Surprise

Ann M. Martin

Illustrations by Susan Tang

A
LITTLE APPLE
PAPERBACK

SCHOLASTIC INC.
New York Toronto London Auckland Sydney

ISBN 0-590-43648-1

12 11 10 9 8 7 6   5/9

Printed in the U.S.A.   28

First Scholastic printing, November 1990

For Susan and Ashley,
who keep my life from being <u>too</u> surprising.
Thank you.

Holidays

"*Hmm, hmm-hmm, hmm, hmmm-hmmm. The pumpkin ran away, before Thanksgiving Day. Said he, 'They'll make a pie of me if I should stay.' Hmm, hmm-hmm.*"

"What's that song?" asked Andrew. Andrew is my little brother. He is four, going on five; I just turned seven.

"It's a Thanksgiving song," I told him. "We're learning about Thanksgiving in school."

"So are we," said Andrew. "Thanksgiving is when you eat a lot."

Oh, Andrew, I thought. That's just what you learn in preschool. There is so much more to Thanksgiving than eating. We had been learning lots of things about the holidays in my school. I was glad. I just love holidays.

My name is Karen Brewer. I have blonde hair and freckles. I wear glasses. I even have two pairs. One pair is for reading and the other pair is for the rest of the time (except when I am asleep). I am in second grade at Stoneybrook Academy. My teacher's name is Ms. Colman. She is gigundo nice. She never yells. And she likes holidays as much as I do. First we celebrated Halloween. We made black cats and pumpkins and ghosts and put them up in our classroom. Yesterday we took them down. Now we are making Thanksgiving decorations. We are making turkeys and Indians and Pilgrims.

"Andrew," I said, "let me tell you what Thanksgiving is *really* about."

"Not food?" asked Andrew. He and I

2

were in the playroom at Mommy's house. We were on the floor, making a town out of blocks. Andrew was in charge of driving toy cars through the town, and sometimes crashing them.

"Yes, it's about food," I answered my little brother. "But it's about other things, too. When we celebrate Thanksgiving, we are remembering the very first people who ever had Thanksgiving. They were called Pilgrims."

"What are Pilgerms?" interrupted Andrew.

"Pil*grims*," I corrected him. "They were some of the first people who lived in America. I mean, except for the Indians. The Indians were already here. They had lived here forever. But then the Pilgrims came from England to find a new home. They had to sail all the way across the ocean. And when they got to America they had to build houses and grow food. But the winter was very, very cold and snowy, so the Indians helped the Pilgrims. Especially two

of the Indians. They were named Samoset and Squanto. They — "

"Squanto!" shrieked Andrew. He began to laugh. "That's a funny name!"

I looked at Andrew. I made my face very serious. "Squanto is an Indian name. Indian names are different from our names. I bet Squanto would think Andrew is a very funny name. I bet Squanto would laugh."

"Really?" said Andrew. He stopped giggling. He crashed two more cars.

Andrew and I played with our town. I built three new houses. "I wonder," I said, looking at the houses, "where we will go for Thanksgiving this year. Mommy's house or Daddy's house."

"Mommy's," said Andrew. "We had Thanksgiving with Daddy last year."

"I know, but then remember Daddy was upset after Christmas? He said that you and I spent Easter *and* Christmas with Mommy last year. Plus we live here most of the time. He said that wasn't fair. He said he wanted the holidays to be different this year. Especially Thanksgiving and Christmas. And Mommy said, 'Okay, we will work something out.' Remember?"

Andrew nodded, but he looked worried.

I tried to cheer him up. "Maybe," I said, "we will have *two* Thanksgivings and *two* Christmases!"

"Yeah!" cried Andrew.

Back and Forth

Here is why Andrew and I might have two Thanksgivings and two Christmases: because our mommy and daddy are divorced. That means that they do not live together anymore. They are not married. They used to be married. That was when they had Andrew and me. I liked our family then. But after awhile, Mommy and Daddy decided that they did not love each other. They still loved Andrew and me, but not each other. So they got a divorce.

And then guess what. They each got

married again! Mommy married a man named Seth. Seth is my stepfather. Daddy married a woman named Elizabeth. Elizabeth is my stepmother. Mommy and Andrew and Seth and I live in a little house. Seth has a cat named Rocky and a dog named Midgie. Andrew and I live with Mommy and Seth most of the time. But every other weekend and for two weeks during the summer, we live with Daddy. It is a good thing that Mommy and Daddy both live in the same town, which is Stoneybrook, Connecticut.

Daddy's house is big. That is another good thing. Why is it good? Because so many people live in it. First of all, there are Daddy and Elizabeth. Then there are Elizabeth's children. She has *four*. They are my stepbrothers and stepsister. Charlie and Sam are old. They go to high school. David Michael is seven, like me. And Kristy is thirteen. I love Kristy! She is one of my favorite people. She is a baby-sitter. She is even the president of a business called the Baby-sitters Club. (Kristy is a gigundo nice

baby-sitter.) Also at the big house is Emily
Michelle. She is my adopted sister. Daddy
and Elizabeth adopted her. She came from
a country called Vietnam. Then there is
Nannie. She is Elizabeth's mother and she
helps take care of Emily Michelle. Let's see,
there are also Shannon and Boo-Boo (David
Michael's puppy and Daddy's fat, mean
cat). And, of course, there are Andrew and
me (sometimes).

Here is another thing. I call myself Karen

Two-Two, and I call my brother Andrew Two-Two. I got the idea from the title of a book Ms. Colman read to our class. It was called *Jacob Two-Two Meets the Hooded Fang*. I think two-two is a good name for Andrew and me because we have two of so many things. We have two houses, the big house and the little house. We have two mommies and two daddies and two dogs and two cats. We each have two bicycles, one at Mommy's and one at Daddy's. (Well, Andrew has two *tri*cycles.) We each have clothes and toys and books and games — at the little house and at the big house. I even have two best friends. Hannie Papadakis lives across the street from Daddy and one house down. Nancy Dawes lives next door to Mommy. Hannie and Nancy and I are all in Ms. Colman's class. We call ourselves the Three Musketeers.

Most of the time I like being a two-two. I like having two houses. I like having two stuffed cats (Moosie at the big house, Goosie at the little house). And I like having Kristy for my big sister. *But* . . . some things about being a two-two are not so good. I only had one special blanket, Tickly. And I kept leaving Tickly at Mommy's or Daddy's house. Finally I had to rip Tickly in half so I could have a piece at each house.

Then there is the problem with holidays. Andrew and I usually switch off holidays. But when Andrew and I are at one house we miss the people at the other house — and they miss us. So this year there were going to be some changes. None of the grown-ups had said a word, though.

What were we going to do about Thanksgiving?

3

A Thanksgiving Celebration

"Okay, boys and girls. Please put your workbooks away," said Ms. Colman.

I slid my workbook in my desk and sat up straight. Ms. Colman had that sound in her voice. It was the sound that meant she was going to make a Surprising Announcement. Ms. Colman is always making Surprising Announcements. That is one reason I like her so much.

It was a Tuesday afternoon. School was almost over for the day. I sneaked a peek at the back of our classroom. I was looking at Hannie and Nancy. They sit in the very last row. I used to sit with them, but when I got my glasses, Ms. Colman moved me to the front row. I sit with Ricky Torres and Natalie Springer. They wear glasses, too. Ricky used to be a pest, but now we like each other. I am glad Ricky sits right next to me.

Anyway, Hannie and Nancy looked excited. They knew a Surprising Announcement was coming. So did Ricky. We waited for Ms. Colman to begin speaking. When she did, she said, "Class, Thanksgiving is just a few weeks away and we are going to do a special project to celebrate the holiday." (Goody! I thought.) "I will write three projects on the board. Then you may vote for one of them."

Here is what Ms. Colman wrote on the board:

1. Fix a Thanksgiving dinner in our classroom. Invite our parents to share it with us.

13

2. Write a story about Thanksgiving. Make the story into a book. Give the book to our school library so that everyone can read it.
3. Put on a play about Thanksgiving.

Oh, boy! I would have a hard time deciding on just one project. Eating Thanksgiving dinner in our classroom sounded like fun. I like to cook. Making a book for our library sounded like fun, too. It would be exciting to be a real author. But putting on a play sounded like *lots* of fun. I just love being in plays. So does Nancy. Nancy is going to be an actress one day. I knew Nancy would vote for the play. I decided to do the same thing. I was sure I would get to be a star in the play.

"Are you ready to vote?" Ms. Colman asked our class.

"Yes!" we cried.

We closed our eyes. We each voted for one project.

14

"Okay," said Ms. Colman. "You may open your eyes. Here are the results. Six people wanted to fix a dinner, four people wanted to write a book, and seven people wanted to put on a play. So we will put on a play."

"Yea!" I cried. (I could not help it.)

"We will put it on for our families and for the students in kindergarten, first grade, second grade, and third grade," added Ms. Colman.

All *right!* I thought. I would have a big audience when I was the star of our play.

When school ended that day, I ran to Hannie and Nancy. "A play! Can you believe it?" I cried.

"This is great!" exclaimed Nancy. "I know I will get a big part in the play. You probably will, too, Karen."

"We better practice our acting, just in case," I said. "We should practice looking happy and sad and excited and scared."

"I can cry real tears whenever I want to," Nancy said.

"You *can?*" I had not known that.

"Yes," said Nancy proudly.

Hmm. I hoped I would do as well as Nancy when we tried out for the play. Ms. Colman had not said anything about tryouts, but I figured I had time to learn how to cry, too.

Turkey Stuffing

"Karen! Dinner!" called Mommy.

"Coming!" I called back. I was in my room playing with my rat. Her name is Emily Junior. I named her after my adopted sister. (That is another bad thing about being a two-two. When I go to Daddy's, I have to leave Emily Junior behind. I miss her.)

I put Emily Junior back in her cage and I ran downstairs. When Andrew and Mommy and Seth and I were sitting in the kitchen and had been served, I said, "Guess what."

"What?" asked everyone.

I could not believe that I had saved up the news about our class play, but I had. I had not told anyone about it all afternoon. Now was the time. "Our class," I began importantly, "is going to put on a Thanksgiving play. We're going to put it on the day before Thanksgiving."

"That's wonderful!" exclaimed Seth.

"Terrific!" added Mommy.

"I'm sure I will have a big part in the play. Nancy, too," I said.

"When will you try out for it?" asked Seth.

"I don't know. Ms. Colman didn't say. I guess as soon as we know what the play will be about. I have to practice my acting. I can look sad, but Nancy can cry *real tears* — whenever she needs to. I bet she will get a bigger part than I will."

"Just do your best," said Mommy.

"I will," I told her. Then I asked, "Will you and Andrew and Seth *and* Daddy and Elizabeth and maybe Nannie and Emily

Michelle come to the play? I really want you all to come and see me."

"We'll try," said Mommy. "I'm sure Seth and I can leave work for an hour or so during the day. Your father and Elizabeth probably can, too."

"Mommy?" spoke up Andrew. "Where are Karen and I going to have Thanksgiving?"

I saw Mommy and Seth look at each other. That is what adults do before they have to tell you something that they don't want to say.

"Well," replied Mommy, "this year everyone wants to celebrate Thanksgiving on Thursday."

"That's when you're supposed to celebrate it," I pointed out.

"Right," said Mommy. "And we all want you and Andrew to celebrate with us. Seth and I want you with us on Thursday, and so do your father and Elizabeth."

Hmm. That was a problem. "So what are we going to do?" I asked.

"You're going to have two Thanksgiving feasts on the same day. First you'll have dinner here. Then you'll go to Daddy's in the afternoon and eat another dinner."

"Two feasts!" I cried. "Two in one day! We'll be as stuffed as turkeys! We will be turkey stuffing!"

"I don't want to be turkey stuffing," said Andrew. He looked like he might cry.

"Don't worry. It will be fun," I told my brother. "I bet not many kids get to have two Thanksgivings in one day. That will be gigundo special."

"It will?" said Andrew.

"I'm sure it will."

After dinner, I was so excited about Thanksgiving that I wanted to tell my friends about it. I picked up the phone in the kitchen. I started to dial Nancy's number. Then I stopped. I did not want to talk to Nancy, and I knew why. I was a little bit mad at her. She could make herself cry, and I could not.

So I called Hannie instead.

"Guess what!" I said. "Andrew and I are going to have Thanksgiving at the little house and Thanksgiving at the big house — all in the same day."

"Karen, you are so lucky!" Hannie replied.

The First Thanksgiving

In school the next day, Ms. Colman said to our class, "What shall our Thanksgiving play be about?"

Six kids shot their hands in the air.

Ms. Colman smiled. "I'm glad that so many of you have ideas, but let me ask you another question. Do we want to write the play ourselves? Writing a play is not easy, but it could be fun."

I remembered to raise my hand.

"Yes, Karen?" said Ms. Colman.

"If we don't write the play, who will?" I asked.

"Miss Kushel's fifth-grade class is interested in writing a play. They could write a Thanksgiving play for us to perform. How many want Miss Kushel's class to write our play?"

Not one hand was raised.

"Okay," said Ms. Colman. "We'll write it ourselves. *Now*, what should our play be about? Pamela?"

Pamela Harding is a new girl in our class. She thinks she is so great because she wears very cool clothes, and her big sister lets her wear her perfume. Also, her father is a dentist and her mother writes books. Most of the girls in our class want to be Pamela's best friend, even though she is a snob. But Hannie and Nancy and I do not like Pamela and she does not like us.

"I think," Pamela began, "that the play should be about all the creatures in the forest having a Thanksgiving dinner."

"Oh, barf," Ricky Torres whispered to me.

But Ms. Colman wrote Pamela's idea on the board. Then she wrote some more ideas on the board. When no one had any more ideas, we voted on the one we liked best. A lot of the girls voted for Pamela's idea, but not enough.

This is the play we voted for. I thought it was a very, very good idea. Natalie Springer thought it up. At the beginning of the play, a family with two parents, three children, and two grandparents are getting ready to celebrate Thanksgiving. On the night before the big day, the older girl in the family falls asleep and dreams that she and her family are Pilgrims. They share the very first Thanksgiving with the Indians. That is the first part of the play. (It is called Act I.) In Act II, the second part of the play, the girl wakes up on Thanksgiving Day. While she helps her family fix the big dinner, the food that they are preparing walks across the stage. That would be fun. We would need costumes that looked like peas and carrots and slices of pie and things.

But the part that I wanted was Samantha, the girl who dreams about the first Thanksgiving. That was the biggest part in the play. Also, it reminded me of a ballet I saw once. It was called *The Nutcracker*. In the story, a little girl named Clara falls asleep on Christmas night and has a very wonderful dream.

"I want to be Samantha," I told Hannie and Nancy on the playground that day.

"Me, too," said Nancy. "It would be just like playing Clara."

"In *The Nutcracker*?" I asked. "That is what I was thinking!"

"I wonder which one of you will get to be Samantha," said Hannie.

"Yeah," I replied. I frowned at Nancy. She was frowning back at me. I did not want her to be Samantha, and she did not want me to be Samantha.

Nancy and I did not talk to each other very much for the rest of recess.

As soon as recess was over, I said to Ms. Colman, "When are we going to have the tryouts for our play?"

"Oh," replied Ms. Colman. "We're not going to have tryouts. We will draw the parts from a hat."

I looked at Nancy with my mouth open. I could not believe what Ms. Colman had just said.

"Who Will Be the
Turkey?"

Nancy and I were friends again right away. There was no reason not to be. We did not have to worry about tryouts anymore. It did not matter that Nancy could cry. And I did not need to learn how to cry. We would not get to show off *any* of our acting skills. Boo.

After school that day, I went to Nancy's house to play.

"I think," Nancy said as she put on a pair of high heels that had been in her dress-up box, "that pulling names out of a hat is silly. What will happen if Natalie gets the part of Samantha? She can't act at all."

"I think it is silly, too," I agreed. (I put a long dress on over my jeans.) "But I guess Ms. Colman knows what she's doing. She wants everyone in our class to have a chance to play a big role. Even the shy kids who might not try out for a big role. She's just being fair."

Nancy sighed. Dressing up was not much fun that day.

We were depressed.

"Tomorrow," said Nancy, sitting on her bed, "we will have the drawing."

"Yeah." I sat down next to her.

"There are seventeen people in our class," Nancy went on. "I will probably not draw Samantha's name out of the hat. You probably won't, either."

"No," I agreed. But then I thought of something. "You know what? One of us *might*. We all have a chance. What if I get

to be Samantha and you don't? Or what if
you get to be Samantha and I don't?''

"Will you be mad if I get to be Samantha?"
asked Nancy.

"I will be sad," I admitted. "But I will
not be mad. Because drawing Samantha's
name will just be luck."

"Maybe you will get to be the other girl
in the family. Melissa. That would be okay."
Nancy paused. "Oh, no! What if one of us

gets to be Samantha and the other one has to be a *vegetable?*"

"It would be awful!" I exclaimed. "Hey, what if a *boy* draws Samantha's name? How could Ricky Torres play Samantha?"

"I think he would have to draw again, for a boy's part," said Nancy.

"Yeah. . . . We'll probably both be vegetables," I added gloomily.

Ms. Colman held the drawing first thing the next morning. I was very, very, very nervous. So was everyone else. Even Pamela Harding.

Before Ms. Colman passed the hat around the room, she said, "Anyone who draws the part of one of the Thanksgiving foods in Act II will also play an Indian in Samantha's dream in Act I. We need Indians. So some of you will play two parts. Are you ready? Then let's begin."

Ricky Torres drew first. He got the part of the grandfather in the family!

Natalie Springer drew second. She was

going to play a pea. And an Indian.

Then darn old Pamela drew, and guess what part she got.

"Samantha! I'm Samantha!" cried Pamela.

I looked at Nancy. I felt like crying.

The drawing continued. When it was all over, Hannie was going to play Samantha's mother, Nancy was going to play a baked potato (and an Indian), and I was going to play . . . the turkey. The *turkey*. (And an Indian, of course.)

"Karen's going to be the *turkey!*" hooted Jannie. (Jannie is one of the girls who hangs around with Pamela now. She says she is Pamela's best friend.)

"Well, Karen *is* a turkey!" said Leslie. (She also thinks she is Pamela's best friend.)

"Karen deserves to be the turkey," added Pamela.

Everyone was laughing.

"Okay, settle down," said Ms. Colman. At least *she* was not laughing.

Neither was Hannie or Nancy. Still, it was a gigundo bad day.

7

The Song of the Vegetables

"It is so, so stupid! It is the stupidest thing I ever heard of!" I cried.

Kristy looked at me seriously. Andrew and I were at the big house for the weekend, and I was telling Kristy about our Thanksgiving play. We were in her room. We were sitting cross-legged on her bed, facing each other.

"Can you believe I have to walk across the stage dressed like a turkey? A *roasted* turkey?"

"Well," said Kristy, "I don't think being

the turkey is so silly. After all, the turkey is the most important part of the Thanksgiving dinner."

"That's true," I replied.

"But I think it's silly that all you have to do is walk across the stage. What will be happening in the play then?"

"Not much. Samantha and her family will be at the back of the stage. They are supposed to be fixing dinner. And every time they say a food — like carrot or turkey or something — the food walks across the stage."

"Well, that is definitely silly," said Kristy. "It seems like such a waste to make all those costumes if the food is just going to walk from one side of the stage to the other. The food parts don't seem very important."

"I know," I replied glumly.

"Maybe you could think of a way to make the food more important. What else could the food do?" asked Kristy.

"Sing?" I suggested.

Kristy did not say anything. Then we both began laughing.

"Singing vegetables!" exclaimed Kristy. When we calmed down, she added, "You know, that isn't a bad idea. In fact, it's a good one."

"Thanks," I said. (Kristy is such a nice big sister.) "I really could write a song for the food. I could write a song about each kind of food and how it is important to the feast."

"That sounds great," Kristy told me.

"The food people could have a whole singing number to themselves. That would show Pamela."

"Picky Pamela?" asked Kristy. (Kristy met Pamela once — when I made the mistake of inviting Pamela to a sleepover party.)

"Yeah, Picky Pamela," I replied. I grinned. "Boy, I better get to work on my song right now. We're going to start writing our play on Monday after recess."

I left Kristy and ran to my room. I sat at my table with a pad of paper and a lot of pencils. Then I put on a baseball cap. I felt like a real writer. I was not sure if I could write a *song*, but at least I could write a poem. If Ms. Colman liked my idea, then maybe my class and I could write the music for it later.

I thought and thought. I decided that sometimes all the food should sing together, but that each kind of food should also have a couple of lines to sing alone. (That is called a solo.) A solo would let everyone feel important. Finally I began to write. This was the beginning of the song:

Hello, hello
And here we come.
We are your Thanksgiving food—
Yum, yum!

That was not bad. Next I wrote some lines for the pumpkin pie, the two cranberries, the squash, the pea, the celery stick, the baked potato, the apple (for the apple pie), the carrot, and finally for me — the turkey.

I wrote the turkey part last. Kristy had said the turkey was the most important food at a Thanksgiving dinner. So I saved the best for last.

I was also getting an idea. It was a wonderful, exciting idea. But I would have to keep it a secret for a long time.

Pecan Pie and Sweet Potatoes

I finished my song after dinner on Saturday. I read it from beginning to end. I liked it so much that I read it again — and again.

I felt very happy with what I had done, so I ran downstairs to find Nannie.

She was reading a book in the living room. "Hi, Nannie," I said.

Nannie looked up. She smiled at me. Then she put her book on a table and patted her lap.

I climbed up. I felt very safe in Nannie's lap.

"I'm coming here on Thanksgiving," I told her. "We can have Thanksgiving together."

"I know," said Nannie. "I'm glad."

"What are we having for Thanksgiving dinner?" I asked.

"Let's see," said Nannie. (She loves to cook.) "Turkey, of course, and peas with little onions, rice, salad, and for dessert, apple pie with ice cream."

"Will there be turkey stuffing?" I asked.

"Definitely," said Nannie.

"Yum. Ooh, Nannie, can you please, please, please make your special sweet potatoes? And a pecan pie? Especially the pie. I *love* pecan pie."

"Okay," agreed Nannie. "Pecan pie. And maybe sweet potatoes."

"Thank you," I said. "Boy, Andrew and I are going to be very busy on Thanksgiving."

"You certainly are."

"You know, we have to watch the Macy's Thanksgiving Day Parade on TV. I hope we

have time to see it before Mommy's dinner. We want to see *all* of it. Especially Santa Claus at the end. Then we will eat our first meal, and *then* we will come over here and eat our second meal."

"Karen," said Nannie, "don't be disappointed if you can't do everything you want to."

"I won't," I said. That was because I was sure Andrew and I would be able to see the parade and then eat two dinners.

"Good girl," said Nannie.

"What are you reading?" I asked her. "Is it a grown-up book?"

"Yes."

"Oh." I like to read, but not grown-up books. "Would you like to hear my poem for the Thanksgiving play?" I asked.

"Of course."

So I read my poem to Nannie. But I did not tell her about my secret idea.

Disney World

On Monday, I had a hard time waiting for recess. We were going to begin working on our play right after recess. And then I could tell Ms. Colman and my friends about the song I had written.

At recess, Hannie and Nancy and I stood by the swings and talked.

"Guess what," said Hannie. (She did not wait for us to guess.) "My grandparents are coming over for Thanksgiving. Our family will be like the family in our play. A mother and a father, two sisters, one brother, and two grandparents. I am so glad my grandparents are coming."

"I don't have any real grandparents," Nancy reminded us. "But Grandma B is coming over." (Grandma B is a grandmother Nancy adopted. She lives at Stoneybrook Manor, which is a home for old people. Grandma B is just as good as a "real" grandma.)

Natalie Springer and Ricky Torres wandered over to us.

"What are you guys talking about?" asked Natalie. Natalie hates being left out of anything.

"Thanksgiving," I replied.

"Oh! Guess where *I* am going for Thanksgiving!" cried Natalie. (She didn't give us time to guess, either.) "I'm going to my cousins' house. They live in Massachusetts. I'll get to spend the night with Uncle Ned and Aunt Rosie and Jeffrey and Sally and Amy."

"*My* cousins are coming to *my* house for Thanksgiving," said Ricky. "Only I don't like them too much. Christopher is three and breaks my things, and Nate is one and cries all the time."

"Too bad," spoke up a voice.

Hannie and Nancy and Ricky and Natalie and I looked around.

There were Pamela and Jannie and Leslie. It was Pamela who had said, "Too bad." But she looked like she did not mean it.

"I," said Pamela, sounding important, "am going to my grandparents' for Thanksgiving."

"Big deal," said Ricky.

"My grandparents live in Florida. Near Disney World." (Leslie and Jannie gave the rest of us big, smug smiles.) "So on Wednesday night we are going to fly to Florida. Then we will have Thanksgiving on Thursday. We will spend Friday and Saturday at . . ." (Pamela paused to make sure she had our attention) "*Disney World.* Then on Sunday we will fly home."

"Ooh," said everyone except me.

I said, "Hmphh. I guess you have not

heard what *I* get to do on Thanksgiving Day."

"What?" asked Natalie.

"I am going to eat *two* dinners. One at my mother's house and one at my father's."

"Two dinners in one *day?*" exclaimed Jannie.

"*Really?*" said Leslie.

"Yup," I replied and sat down on a swing. I felt pleased with myself. Everybody thought

that two dinners in one day was much more unusual than going to Disney World.

Well, Pamela did not think so. She just said, "You'll get fat."

Jannie and Leslie laughed. Natalie did not know whether to laugh or not.

I said, "I've already been to Disney World. I don't need to go again. But, Pamela, you know what the best ride at Disney World is?"

"What?" asked Pamela.

"Space Mountain. It is a *wild* roller coaster. I think you should go on that ride first. But make sure that before you do, you eat a huge snack."

Everybody laughed. Even Leslie and Jannie. They were all laughing at what I had said to Pamela.

Karen's Good Idea

As soon as recess was over, Ms. Colman said to our class, "Okay, everybody. Settle down. We have work to do."

Pamela was still mad at me for making fun of her trip to Disney World. Especially after Ricky told her she would be a barf-face if she rode on Space Mountain. She kept calling me a turkey.

But when Ms. Colman said, "Settle down," we settled down.

"Now," Ms. Colman went on, "we will

begin writing our play. We all know what the play is about. Who can think of a way to begin it?"

My hand shot up.

"Yes, Karen?"

"Well, I don't have a way to begin the play — "

"Turkey!" whispered Pamela to Leslie. She pointed at me.

" — but I have an idea for Act II. See, I was thinking that the people who are going to play food, like *turkeys*," I said, turning around to look at Pamela, "should have bigger parts. All we have to do right now is walk across the stage. I think we will be wasting our costumes. So I wrote a song for the food. Well, it's just a poem now, but we can make it into a song. Everybody would get a solo in the song, and sometimes we would all sing together."

"Class?" said Ms. Colman. "What do you think of Karen's idea? Would you like to hear her poem?"

"Yes!" cried a lot of voices. (I think they were the food voices.) So I began to read my poem.

Hello, hello
And here we come.
We are your Thanksgiving food —
Yum, yum!

I am a cranberry!
So am I!
I am a pumpkin,
So I'll be the pie!

I read all the verses to my poem. When I finished, the food people began to clap. So did some of the others. (Not Pamela, of course.) And Ms. Colman was smiling.

"I'm glad I'm a cranberry now," said Hank Reubens.

"*I'm* glad *I'm* a pea," said Natalie.

"I can't wait to sing my baked potato song!" exclaimed Nancy.

Wow, I thought. Kristy had been right.

Everyone just needed to feel more important.

"How many people want to use Karen's song in our play?" asked Ms. Colman.

Eleven hands were raised. That was more than half of our class!

"Fine," said Ms. Colman. "I think I'll ask Mrs. Noonan" (she is our music teacher) "if she can turn Karen's poem into a song. And then I'll ask Mrs. Brown" (she is one of our gym teachers) "if she can make up a dance to go with the song."

A song-and-dance number! I could not believe it!

I guess Nancy could not, either. She called out excitedly, "Ms. Colman! Ms. Colman! That is perfect because I take dancing lessons!"

Pamela slouched in her seat. She would not get to sing or dance in the play. And I knew she wanted to.

We worked on our play for awhile. Then Ms. Colman handed each of us a piece of paper. On the paper were descriptions of

the costumes we would need. (We were in charge of making our own costumes. Our parents were allowed to help.)

When school was over, Pamela whispered, *"Tur-key,"* in my ear. I did not care anymore.

Olives and Hot Apple Cider

"Karen, hold still," said Mommy. Only it sounded like she said, "Kem, hode stiw." That was because her mouth was full of pins.

Mommy was working on my costume. It was a Tuesday evening. Dinner was over. I had finished my homework. And Mommy had said, "Karen, I've been sewing your turkey costume. Tonight I need you to try it on. I need to measure some things."

So I was standing on a chair in the kitchen. I was wearing a boring, old brown costume.

My arms were going to be cooked, brown turkey wings, and my legs were going to be cooked, brown turkey drumsticks. But my head was going to stick out of the top of the costume. I thought that was silly. Turkeys don't have people heads with blonde hair.

But I did not say that to Mommy. She had already helped me put together my Indian costume. Now she was making the turkey suit by herself. She said it was very hard.

"Mommy? What are we going to have for Thanksgiving dinner?" I asked her.

Mommy took the pins out of her mouth. "We will have turkey and butternut squash and wild rice and cranberry relish. And for dessert we will have baked apples with cream and a pumpkin pie."

"That's a lot of food for four people!" I said.

"I think it's nice to have a choice of food to eat on Thanksgiving," Mommy replied. "You don't have to eat everything."

I thought for a moment. Then I asked, "Can we have olives at dinner, too? I want the black kind, the ones with *no* pits, and also the green kind with the red stuff in them. We can put them in the special olive dish."

"Maybe," said Mommy. "We'll see."

"And can we also have your special apple cider? The hot kind? With the cinnamon sticks floating in it? Puh-*lease*?"

"Do you really like my hot apple cider?" asked Mommy.

"I *love* it!"

"Then I'll make it. I'll get the olives, too."

"Oh, thank you! And you know what else? Andrew and I have to see the Thanksgiving parade before dinner. We want to see the whole thing, so we can see Santa Claus at the end."

"Honey, I don't know about that," said Mommy. "We have to eat early. You and Andrew need time to go to Daddy's and get your tummies ready for another big meal."

"But we've *got* to see Santa!" I cried. "We see him every year. If we have to start dinner before the parade is over, can we eat in front of the TV?"

"Absolutely not," replied Mommy. "We will eat in the dining room."

"Then maybe," I said, "I don't want to eat two meals in one day."

Mommy stopped working. She looked up at me and smiled. But it was a sad smile.

"I'm not sure I would want to eat two Thanksgiving dinners in one day, either. Especially if I wanted to watch the parade. But this is the arrangement that Daddy and I came up with. I'm sorry, sweetie."

I tried to smile back. I thought about being the only kid in my class who would have two Thanksgivings. That was special. I thought about singing and dancing in our school play. I thought about my surprise.

Then I really did smile.

"Can I go look in the mirror?" I asked Mommy. "I want to see how my costume is coming." Mommy let me hop off the chair. Then I stood in front of the bathroom mirror. My costume was great. I would be the best turkey ever!

12

Rehearsing

Only six more days until Thanksgiving! Only five more days until our play!

It was the Friday before Thanksgiving and we were going to have a rehearsal for our play. Everyone's costumes were finished, or almost finished. So guess what. We were going to have a *dress* rehearsal. And we were going to hold it on the *stage* in our school auditorium.

"Do you all understand what a *dress* rehearsal is?" asked Ms. Colman.

We were still in our classroom. We were sitting in our seats. We had not put on our costumes yet.

"Yes!" cried several of my friends — and me.

"No!" cried everyone else.

"A dress rehearsal," Ms. Colman began, "is when you rehearse in your costumes. And you try to put on the play from beginning to end without stopping, even if you make mistakes."

"Okay," we said.

Then Ms. Colman led us to the auditorium. She took us backstage (behind the curtain) and we put our costumes on over our school clothes. The food people put their Indian outfits on.

"Ready?" asked Ms. Colman.

"Ready," we said.

Ms. Colman opened the curtain. Ricky, Hannie, and the others who were playing Samantha's family walked onto the stage. They were busy in the kitchen. (Our art

teacher, Mr. Mackey, had helped us draw scenery that looked like a kitchen.) Then Samantha skipped onstage.

"Hello, Mom! Hello, Dad!" she said.

"Pamela is the worst actress I have ever seen," I whispered to Nancy.

"I know," Nancy replied.

"Um, what comes next?" asked Pamela.

I snickered.

"Pamela, you should know your lines by now," said Ms. Colman.

Just then, Ricky's white-haired grandfather wig fell off. And Hannie leaned against a fake stove. The stove fell over and so did Hannie.

Ms. Colman closed her eyes for a moment.

"I really don't remember my next line," said Pamela.

I snickered again. I couldn't help it. Pamela's next line was, "Hello, Melissa."

How stupid can you get?

Unfortunately, Jannie heard me snickering. "*Tur-key!*" she said.

I did not even look at her. I would show

59

her. I was going to be a great Indian *and* a great turkey — if Pamela ever remembered her lines so we could get on with the play.

It seemed like forever, but *finally* Samantha (Pamela) fell asleep and began dreaming. All the Indians rushed onstage. Jannie said Leslie's line, and Leslie said Jannie's line, but *I* said my lines perfectly. (I had three of them.)

At last Act I was over. Act II began. The food filed onto the stage in rows. I got to stand in the middle of the front row since I was the turkey. But I didn't get to sing my solo until the end. Then I sang, *"And last of all, look at me! I am your special Thanksgiving turkey!"*

Mrs. Noonan played the piano.

When our rehearsal was over, Ms. Colman said, "I think this needs a little work. Pamela, you *must* memorize your lines." But then she added, "Karen and Nancy, nice work."

I beamed. I was going to be the hit of our play.

Play Day

Play day finally arrived. I woke up excited. I could not wait to star in the play. Plus, the next day would be . . . Thanksgiving! My special Thanksgiving.

Our class was going to put on our play after recess. The kindergartners, first-graders, second-graders, and third-graders would be in the audience. So would Mommy and Seth, Daddy and Elizabeth, Andrew, Emily, and Nannie. And of course a lot of other parents and younger brothers and sisters.

We had held two more rehearsals since

the gigundo bad one on Friday. The last one had been much better. Pamela knew her lines (pretty well). Ricky's wig did not fall off anymore. And we all knew not to lean on the scenery.

Even so, I woke up feeling excited *and* nervous on Wednesday. What if I made a mistake in front of everybody? What if I knocked something over? Maybe I should not have laughed at Pamela when she forgot her lines.

But when I reached school, I discovered something. I was not the only one with butterflies in my tummy.

"I am a little nervous," Nancy said as we stood together in our classroom.

"Me too," said Natalie.

"Me three," said Hannie.

"Me four," I admitted.

"What if I do something stupid?" asked Nancy. "What if I trip while I'm dancing? What if I forget my line?" (Nancy had one line in her role as an Indian.)

"Don't talk about those things," I replied. "It might be bad luck."

So we stopped talking about the play. But we could not stop thinking about it.

In the morning, we worked at our desks.

"Hmm hmm-hmm-hmm, look at me," I sang softly.

"Quit it," said Ricky. "I can't work if you make noise."

"Sorry," I replied. *"Hmm hmm-hmm — "*

"*Quit* it!"

"Ricky? Karen?" said Ms. Colman. "Please settle down."

I tried to. But before I knew it I was humming again.

"Cut . . . it . . . *out!*" hissed Ricky. "I can't think!"

"Karen?" said Ms. Colman. "Do you need to sit somewhere else this morning?"

"No," I answered.

I managed to keep quiet until lunchtime. By then, those butterflies were really fluttering around in my stomach. I didn't eat much. Neither did a lot of kids in my class. And at recess, we just stood around. Can you believe it? We wanted recess to be *over*. Usually, recess is so, so fun.

But at last we were in the auditorium, behind the stage. The girls changed on one side and the boys changed on the other side.

"I know the boys are going to peek at us," Natalie whispered to me.

"Don't think about that. Think about your lines," I told her.

"No," said Natalie. "That's worse. Gosh, I wonder how many people are here." Natalie had finished putting on her costume. She peeked through the curtain. "There are *thousands* of people out there!" she cried.

I gulped.

Hannie and Nancy looked scared.

But Pamela did not. She brushed her hair. She smiled at Leslie and Jannie. Then she whispered, *"Tur-key,"* to me, even though I was wearing my Indian costume.

"Stupid-head," I replied.

I think Pamela wanted to say something back to me, but just then Ms. Colman appeared. "Are you ready?" she asked. "The curtain is going to go up. Places, everyone."

14

Karen's Thanksgiving Surprise

Ooh, I was so scared. All us Indians stood in the wings. We watched the curtain go up. When it did, this is what the audience saw:

The kids who were playing Samantha's parents, grandparents, brother, and sister were on the stage. They were pretend cooking pretend food in the pretend kitchen. Then Samantha (Pamela) skipped onto the stage. She greeted everyone. Act I had begun.

Can you believe it? Hardly anyone made

a mistake. Once, Pamela said "bancrerry" when she meant "cranberry," but the other actresses and actors pretended not to notice. That was what Ms. Colman had told us to do.

Soon Pamela fell asleep and dreamed about the first Thanksgiving. The other Indians and I ran onstage.

I got to say my lines. They were: "We come in peace," and, "Here is some nice maize," (maize is corn), and, "A happy Thanksgiving to all!" (I had written that line myself.)

When Act I ended, the audience applauded. The Indians and I had to change into our food costumes fast. We had to be ready for our big number in Act II. This was our cue to run onto the stage again: Pamela said, "And now our wonderful Thanksgiving food is all ready!"

Pamela, Ricky, Hannie, and the other kids stood at the back of the stage. The food ran on. We began our number. At first, we all sang and danced together. Then we got to

67

take turns. The pumpkin pie sang, the cranberries sang, the squash sang, and the pea sang. Some parts were complicated. We had to remember that we *all* sang, *"What are you, you tall green stick?"* Then just the celery sang, *"I am celery,"* and *then* the rest of us sang, *"Ew, ew, yick!"* (None of us like celery too much.)

My part came last. By then, I was feeling comfortable. I could tell that the audience liked the food song — a lot. So I knew they would like my surprise. Right in time with the piano, I sang, *"And last of all, look at me! I am your special Thanksgiving turkey!"*

That was supposed to be the end of the song. But I did not stop singing. Nobody knew that I had written three more turkey verses for myself. I kept right on singing and dancing. Mrs. Noonan did not know what to do. She had to stop playing the piano. I was on my own. Everyone was looking at me.

I was a star.

Actually, I do not think that Ms. Colman

was very happy. She gave me a sharp look. And once, when I was twirling around, I saw Pamela behind me. She was glaring at me. So what. I was putting my boring brown turkey costume to good use.

When I finished my special solo, I slid one knee (a drumstick) onto the floor and flapped my wings in the air. The audience clapped and clapped. Then the dancing food ran offstage.

"Karen!" exclaimed Nancy in a whisper. "What was that?"

"My Thanksgiving surprise," I replied. I smiled happily.

"I bet Ms. Colman is going to be mad."

"Ms. Colman never gets mad. At least, she never yells. Anyway, maybe she will be too busy to get mad."

I looked at Ms. Colman, who was directing the very last part of the play. In that part, Samantha and her family ate their Thanksgiving dinner. When they were finished, they joined hands and took a bow. Then they stood back while the food came

onstage again. We held hands and ran out in one long line. Then, still holding hands, we bowed.

We got more applause than Samantha and the other kids did.

Our play was over. I was no longer a *turkey*.

The Beginning

The curtain came down.

"We did it!" cried Nancy.

"Yeah, we did it!" I replied.

Everyone began taking off their costumes. But before I could get out of my turkey suit, I heard someone say, "Karen? May I see you for a moment?"

It was Ms. Colman.

Uh-oh, I thought. She *is* mad. I wonder if she will yell after all. It would be the first time. *Please* don't yell too loudly, I wanted to tell her.

But Ms. Colman did not yell. She led me away from the other kids. Then she said, "Karen, you really put on a show."

"Thank you," I answered.

"But do you know that you should not have put it on?"

I didn't say anything.

"You cannot always be the star," Ms. Colman told me. "You almost messed up the play. I understand that being the turkey was not easy for you. But when you did

something that we had not rehearsed, you confused Mrs. Noonan. You confused the kids who were on the stage with you. You confused me. That wasn't fair. You might have ruined the play."

"I'm sorry," I said. And I meant it.

"Will you promise me something? No more surprises?" asked Ms. Colman.

"I promise," I said.

But even as I said it, people were starting to come backstage. They wanted to talk to me. They wanted to congratulate me.

"You were wonderful, Karen!" exclaimed Mrs. Papadakis.

"I didn't know you could dance so well!" said Mr. Dawes.

"You were a hit!" cried Daddy. Even my family did not know that I was only supposed to have a regular verse to sing.

My friends were not quite so happy with what I had done.

"Stage-hog!" said Hank Reubens.

"Yeah," said Natalie, who does not usually get mad. She cries sometimes, and then she snorts. But she is not usually angry. "You said you wrote that song so the food parts would be more important. Then you gave your*self* the biggest part. And you did not even tell anybody. That wasn't fair."

Pamela must have liked the sound of "stage-hog," because she sang it over and over. *"Stage-hog! Stage-hog! Karen is a stage-hog!"*

"You are just mad because people didn't like you as much as they liked me!" I said.

"Oh, who cares?" replied Pamela. "In two days I will be at Disney World."

"You'll be a barf-face," I reminded her.

This time a bunch of kids giggled. Only Leslie and Jannie did not.

Oh, well. It was time to go home. School was over. Our play was over. But I was not sad. The next day would be Thanksgiving. And Thanksgiving, I think, is the beginning of . . . Christmas. When Thanksgiving comes, the stores start to put up lights. They decorate fir trees in their windows. On TV, you see Santa Claus in lots of commercials. Mommy and Seth and Daddy and Elizabeth begin to hide packages. In school, we make snowflakes and bells and stars to put up on our walls. And dreidels and menorahs for Hanukkah. It is my favorite season of the year.

"Come on, Karen," said Mommy. "Find your clothes. It's time to go home."

So I left Stoneybrook Academy with Mommy and Seth and Andrew.

I was gigundo excited about Thanksgiving.

Thanksgiving at the
Little House

"It's Thanksgiving! It's Thanksgiving!" I cried when I woke up the next morning.

I hopped out of bed.

What a great day! It was a holiday. It was the first day of a school vacation. It was the beginning of Christmas.

I had decided that I would not eat breakfast. I wanted to be good and hungry for Mommy's big dinner. So I did not run downstairs like I usually do on a day off from school. Instead, I dressed in my party clothes. I put on my green velvet dress with the white lace collar, and white tights, and my black Mary Janes. Soon I will be old enough to wear shoes that do *not* have straps and buckles on them.

I went downstairs.

"There's my girl," said Seth. He kissed me good morning. "You look beautiful."

"Thank you," I said.

But Mommy did not say I looked beautiful. She was arguing with Andrew. She wanted Andrew to wear his suit and tie. Andrew wanted to wear blue jeans.

Mommy won the argument.

Later that morning, Andrew and I were sitting on the couch in front of the TV. We were watching the Macy's Thanksgiving Day Parade. We were so dressed up that Seth had taken four pictures of us.

We watched the balloons in the parade. The balloons are our favorites.

"There's Snoopy!" I said.

"There's Superman!" cried Andrew.

Soon the parade was almost over. We were watching a bunch of people dressed as elves dancing in the street. Santa would come along at any moment. I could smell turkey and cranberry sauce and other good things coming from our kitchen.

Ding-dong! went the doorbell.

"I wonder who that could be," I said to Andrew.

I said it just as Seth called, "Karen! Andrew! Answer the door, please!"

"But we don't want to miss Santa Claus!" I called back.

"Mommy and I are busy. Please get the door," said Seth.

So Andrew and I ran to the door. We wanted to answer it fast.

Guess who was there. It was Granny and Grandad. They had come all the way from the state of Nebraska!

"Surprise!" they cried.

"Surprise!" said Mommy and Seth from behind us. "Look who's here!"

Granny and Grandad are Seth's parents. Andrew and I love them very much. They live on a farm with animals.

Everybody hugged and hugged. Then Andrew and I raced to the TV just in time to see Santa. "There he is!" cried Andrew.

"Merry Christmas!" I added.

Ding-dong! went the doorbell.

"Again?" said Andrew.

This time we answered it without being told. And there were Grandma and Grandpa Packett — Mommy's parents! (They live here in Stoneybrook.)

There was more hugging. And Mommy and Seth said, "Surprise!" again. There were going to be *eight* people for Thanksgiving. I had been so busy watching the parade that I had not noticed the four extra places Seth set at the dining-room table. (Now I knew why Mommy had made so much food.)

Anyway, we started eating as soon as Grandma and Grandpa Packett took off their coats. First we drank the special hot apple cider in the living room. Then we sat down at the table for dinner.

I was starving, since I had not eaten breakfast.

"Save room for dinner at Daddy's," Mommy said to me.

I tried to, but Mommy's food was good.

By the time we left for the big house, I was sort of full.

Thanksgiving at the Big House

Before Andrew and I could ring the bell at the big house, the door opened wide.

"Happy Thanksgiving!" There were Daddy, Elizabeth, Kristy, Charlie, Sam, David Michael, Nannie, and Emily Michelle.

"Happy Thanksgiving!" cried Andrew and I. Then I turned around. " 'Bye, Mommy!" I called.

" 'Bye!" she replied. "I'll be back around six o'clock." She drove away.

When Andrew and I walked inside the

big house we smelled all sorts of good things. There was more turkey, of course, and I thought I could smell onions and apple pie and even the pecan pie!

"Mmm," I said. "Yum!"

Kristy helped Andrew take his coat off, and I handed her mine.

"Don't you guys look nice," she said.

Andrew scowled and tugged at his collar.

I fanned out my dress and said, "Thank you."

Then everybody — all ten people — went into the living room. My big house family was dressed up, too. Especially Emily. She was wearing a new party outfit. It was a red dress with smocking on the front. She was also wearing a big red headband, and white tights and Mary Jane shoes like mine.

"Happy Thanksgiving, Emily," I said. (It was her very first Thanksgiving.)

"Turkey!" replied Emily. I was not sure if she meant dinner or me.

"I'm starving," announced Sam.

"Then I will bring out the cheese and crackers," said Nannie. "But we can't eat dinner for awhile. Karen and Andrew just ate at their mother's house."

"Oh," groaned Sam.

And David Michael moaned, "I can't wait. I'm hungry now."

I looked at Andrew. I felt bad. I could tell that he felt bad, too. We were holding up dinner at the big house. Everyone had to wait because of us.

But then Nannie said, "Besides, the turkey isn't ready yet." So we felt better.

Andrew and I did not eat any cheese and crackers. But everyone else did. They managed to wait until four o'clock. Then Nannie said, "Turkey's ready!"

"Yea!" cried David Michael.

"It's about time," muttered Sam.

I held Andrew's hand as we walked into the dining room. We sat next to each other. Andrew was sorry he had made Sam angry. Also, he was still full.

So was I. But when I saw all the wonderful food that Daddy and Elizabeth and Nannie brought to the table, I thought I might be able to eat another meal.

Andrew could not eat. He just picked. (No one cared.)

But I ate more turkey and the peas with onions and the rice and of course some of the sweet potatoes. (I skipped the salad, though.)

By the time we were clearing the table, I was very, very full. I was a stuffed turkey.

Maybe Nannie felt the same way, because she said, "Let's take a break before we eat dessert."

But Sam replied, "Do we have to? I'm still hungry." (Sam could eat up the dining room and still be hungry.)

"Who wants dessert now?" asked Nannie.

"Me!" said almost everybody. (But not Andrew and I.)

Even so, when Nannie brought those pies out, I said, "Oh, boy!"

Andrew did not eat dessert. But I ate a piece of pecan pie with ice cream on top. I could not help it. Then — "Daddy?" I said as I pushed my plate away. "I don't feel so good."

18

Karen's Stomachache

"What's the matter?" Daddy asked me. He jumped up from his place at the table.

"My stomach hurts," I said.

"Are you going to barf?" asked David Michael. He looked really interested.

"No," I said. "But my stomach hurts a *lot*." I began to cry.

"Oh, Karen," said Daddy. "I think you ate too much. Come here."

Daddy held out his arms. I let him pick me up and carry me to my bedroom in the big house. Then I lay down. I hugged Moosie and Tickly.

"Let me get you something for your tummy," said Daddy.

"No," I moaned. "I don't want anything. Not even medicine. I'm too full."

"Okay," replied Daddy. "Maybe you can fall asleep. Maybe you'll feel better after a nap."

"Okay," I said. But I knew I would not fall asleep. My stomach hurt too much. So

I just lay on my bed. Sometimes I clutched Moosie and Tickly. Sometimes I clutched my stomach. I tried not to wrinkle my party dress.

Once, Kristy came in. "How do you feel?" she asked.

"Not too good," I said honestly.

"Andrew is all tired out," Kristy told me. "He fell asleep on the couch in the living room. Everyone was talking and laughing, and Andrew fell sound asleep."

I tried to smile.

"I guess I'll let you rest," said Kristy. "Your mom will be here soon."

After Kristy left, I listened to the sounds in the big house. I heard Elizabeth say, "Uh-oh, Emily!" Then she brought her upstairs and changed her out of her new clothes and into a pair of overalls.

I heard Charlie shout, "All *right!* Touchdown!" He was probably in the den. He said there was going to be a good football game on TV that afternoon.

I heard dishes clattering and knew that

somebody was cleaning the kitchen.

At last I heard, *Honk, honk!* Mommy had come. She was waiting for Andrew and me to run out to the car. But neither of us could. I heard the front door open, and then I heard Daddy call, "Lisa?" (That's Mommy.) "Can you come in for a minute?"

When I heard the front door close, I knew Mommy was inside. But I just could not get up. I was pretty sure Daddy was telling her that I did not feel well and that Andrew was asleep.

She might have to wait awhile before she could take us home.

It would serve her right, I thought. The grown-ups had ruined Thanksgiving.

Never Again

I lay around on my bed for awhile longer. Finally I heard Andrew say sleepily, "Hi, Mommy." I decided I felt well enough to get up. So I laid Moosie and Tickly on my bed. "See you guys next weekend," I told them.

Then I went downstairs. I walked very carefully, because my stomach still hurt. But it did not hurt as much as before.

"Karen!" said Mommy when she saw me. She was sitting in the living room with

Daddy and Elizabeth and Nannie and Andrew. She does not like to spend time with Elizabeth. They feel uncomfortable when they are together. It was nice of Mommy to wait for me.

"How are you feeling?" she asked me.

"A little better," I said in a sad voice.

"Poor pumpkin," said Mommy. "Come sit on my lap."

"Okay," I replied. "But don't say any more food words."

Everyone laughed.

Then Andrew climbed onto Daddy's lap, and Daddy said, "I think we need to have a talk."

"What did I do wrong?" asked Andrew.

"Nothing." Daddy smiled. "I meant, I think we *all* need to have a talk. Thanksgiving didn't work out very well, did it?"

"No way," I answered. "I am never going to eat again in my whole life."

"Never?" asked Andrew, wide-eyed. "Not even dessert?"

"Not even dessert. And especially not turkey," I added.

"That's okay," said Nannie.

"I'm still tired," Andrew announced.

"This day," said Mommy, "has been too much for Karen and Andrew."

"Much too much," I agreed.

"Do we have to do this again next year?" asked Andrew. "I hope not, because I don't want to."

"Neither do I," I said. "*Please* can we do something different? I don't ever, ever want to have two celebrations on the same day. Not two birthdays, not two Easters, not two Christmases, and especially not two Thanksgivings."

"I would like to open presents on Christmas Eve at one house, and on Christmas Day at the other house," said Andrew.

"Me, too," I said. "That spreads things out. Why can't we have one Thanksgiving on Thursday next year, and another one on Friday?" I asked.

"I think you will," Mommy answered. She glanced at Daddy and he nodded.

"Why did we have to have two Thanksgivings today?" asked Andrew. "I forget."

"Because . . . because we were all being a little selfish," Elizabeth spoke up. "At least, the adults were. Your daddy and I wanted Thanksgiving on Thursday."

"And so did Seth and I," said Mommy. "Especially since your grandparents were coming. I guess we didn't think how you and Andrew would feel."

"Do you promise that we'll never do this again?" I asked.

"Never again," said Daddy.

"Thank you." I sighed.

"We better go now," said Mommy. So Daddy got our coats. He carried Andrew to the car. I walked outside, holding Mommy's hand.

On the way back to the little house, Mommy said, "Guess what. Granny and Grandad are staying until Sunday."

"Oh, goody!" exclaimed Andrew and I together. Then I added, "Nancy can finally meet Granny." (Granny and Nancy are pen pals. They write letters to each other. But they have never met. It's a long story.)

By the time we got home, I was asleep.

It Isn't Easy Being a Two-Two

Thanksgiving vacation was over.

It was Monday. School had started again. I did not mind, of course. Now it was the Christmas season. I could not wait to decorate our classroom.

I was relieved that Thanksgiving was over. My stomachache was gone. I was eating again (even though I had told Andrew I never would). But I wanted to forget Thanksgiving Day.

"It was awful," I had said to Nancy on the day after Thanksgiving.

And, "It was terrible," I had told Hannie over the phone.

Everyone else had had great Thanksgivings. Before school started, my friends and I talked about them.

"I had so much fun with my grandparents," said Hannie. "They brought presents for Linny and Sari and me."

"We had Grandma B over," announced Nancy. "After dinner we sang songs and Grandma B played the piano."

I did not say that after dinner all I did was get a stomachache.

Ricky said, "My cousins weren't so bad after all. Christopher didn't break anything, and Nate only cried when he had to leave."

"I had a sleepover with my cousins," said Natalie. "On Thanksgiving night we stayed up until midnight. Then we snuck into the kitchen and made turkey sandwiches. Our parents — "

"Well, I'm back!" someone interrupted Natalie.

It was Pamela, of course. And of course,

Leslie and Jannie were with her.

Pamela took off her coat. She was wearing a new outfit. It was a flowered jumpsuit. But best of all, on her head were Mickey Mouse ears. *Pamela* was written on them in gold wiggly cursive.

"I brought presents for my friends," said Pamela.

"You did?" I cried.

"Yup." Pamela pulled some more Mickey Mouse ears out of a bag. The first pair said

Jannie. The second pair said *Leslie.* She had not brought hats for anyone else.

Leslie and Jannie put their ears on and smiled. Pamela said, "Disney World was so, so fun. We did *every*thing. We went on Mr. Toad's Wild Ride, and we went in the castle, and we went to Frontierland and Epcot Center. *And* I went on Space Mountain three times and I did not get sick." Pamela gave Ricky and me a Look.

I inched closer to Hannie and Nancy. We were still the Three Musketeers, even if we did not have matching hats like Pamela, Leslie, and Jannie.

"Well," I began, "my *two* Thanksgivings were gigundo fun. My brother and I watched the parade on TV, right to the end. My grandparents came as a *surprise.* Four of them. And Granny and Grandad brought *presents.* And, let's see. Since I had *two* dinners, I got to eat lots of desserts. I had a baked apple and three kinds of pie." (Not all of this was true.) "It was a wonderful day."

Everyone looked at me.

"Lucky duck," said Leslie. (Pamela punched her arm.)

I glanced at Hannie and Nancy. They knew how my Thanksgiving had really been. But they would not tell. They are my best friends, and best friends keep secrets.

There was one secret that I had not told even Nancy and Hannie, though. This is the secret:

Sometimes it isn't easy being a Two-Two.

About the Author

ANN M. MARTIN lives in New York City and loves animals. Her cat, Mouse, knows how to take the phone off the hook.

Other books by Ann M. Martin that you might enjoy are *Stage Fright*, *Me and Katie (the Pest)*, and the books in *The Baby-sitters Club* series.

Ann likes ice cream, the beach, and *I Love Lucy*. And she has her own little sister, whose name is Jane.

Little Sister

Don't miss #14

KAREN'S NEW YEAR

Daddy served me eggs and fruit and a muffin. "What do you want to drink?" he asked. "You can have anything you want."

Before I could answer, we all heard a loud "B-U-R-P!"

"Excuse me," said Sam.

"Sam!" I cried. "You already broke your New Year's resolution! You didn't keep it for a day. You didn't keep it at *all*. This is your first meal of the new year. And you burped."

"*Sorry*," said Sam. (He did not sound very sorry.)

"Okay, okay," said Daddy. "Enough arguing."

I didn't say anything else to Sam during brunch — even though he did not burp again. But I had a plan.